**For Lisa, the best player on my team**

First edition 2008

Library of Congress Cataloging-in-Publication Data is available.

Library of Congress Catalog Card Number 2007940976

ISBN 978-0-7636-3390-5

2 4 6 8 10 9 7 5 3 1

Printed in Singapore

This book was typeset in Avenir Black.
The illustrations were created digitally.

Candlewick Press
2067 Massachusetts Avenue
Cambridge, Massachusetts 02140

visit us at www.candlewick.com

# BIG KICKS

## Bob Kolar

CANDLEWICK PRESS
CAMBRIDGE, MASSACHUSETTS

IN A QUIET LITTLE CORNER of a busy little town
lived a very large bear. His name was Biggie.

Biggie spent a lot of time by himself, playing jazz, eating peanut-butter-and-banana sandwiches, and working on his amazing stamp collection.

One Saturday morning, there was a knock on Biggie's door.

It was the town soccer team.
"Hello," said Biggie. "May I help you?"

"I can't ask him," said Chicken Rabbit. "I'm too afraid."
"I can't ask him," said Twirly Squirrel. "I'm too little."
"I can't ask him," said Smelly Smell Skunk. "I'm too stinky."
"I forgot what to ask him," said Fluff the Duck.
 Poke the Turtle stepped up.

"We are the Mighty Giants," said Poke. "We have a big game today, and Brown Dog came down with fleas."

"We need someone with a big kick," said Twirly Squirrel.
"We need someone big and brave," said Chicken Rabbit.
"We need someone with a big brain," said Fluff the Duck.
"We need someone who doesn't stink," said Smelly Smell Skunk.

**"We need a big bear!"** they said together.

"But I've never played soccer before," said Biggie.

"Don't worry. You're big, and the ball is little," said Twirly Squirrel.

"Well, I do look good in red," said Biggie.

"Let's go!" said Chicken Rabbit.

The Screaming Pirates were warming up when the Mighty Giants arrived.

"This is Biggie," said Poke. "He's on *our* team."

"Hello," said Biggie.
"Uh-oh," said the Pirates.

The game started with a big kick from Biggie.

But he missed the ball!

BA-DUMP!

When Biggie tried to get to the ball, someone got there first.
When Biggie tried to kick the ball, it went the wrong way.
When Biggie tried to stop the ball, it flew right by him.

Maybe being big and being good at soccer were not the same.

The game was almost over and the score was tied.
Then something amazing happened.

Biggie saw a very rare, twenty-four-cent, never-been-used, upside-down, special-delivery postage stamp!

He bent down to scoop it up and—

BONK!

The ball bounced off Biggie's head.

It bounced over his teammates.

It bounced around

The Giants yelled, "We won the game!"
The Pirates yelled, "We lost the game!"

Biggie yelled, "I found a very rare, twenty-four-cent, never-been-used, upside-down, special-delivery postage stamp!"

The team tried to carry Biggie off the field—
but they couldn't.

"I want to go home," said Biggie.
"It's time for a party!" cheered Chicken Rabbit.
"I have to add this to my collection," said Biggie.
"Party at Biggie's house!" shouted Fluff the Duck.

"What about snacks?" asked Poke the Turtle.
"What about music?" asked Twirly Squirrel.
"What do you do with a stinky old postage stamp?" asked Smelly Smell Skunk.

"Follow me," said Biggie.

Biggie threw a great party.
They ate peanut-butter-and-banana sandwiches,
played jazz, and told exciting stories about soccer
and stamp collecting.

Now Biggie loves going to every game.
He's still a special part of the team—
he's the Mighty Giants' biggest fan.